ANNIE LUMSDEN,
the Girl from the Sea

For Julia
DA

For Olimpia and Mimosa, my little girls from the sea
BA

Text copyright © 2007 by David Almond
Previously published as "Half a Creature from the Sea"
in *Click* and *Half a Creature from the Sea: A Life in Stories*
Illustrations copyright © 2020 by Beatrice Alemagna

First US edition 2021
First published by Walker Books Ltd. (UK) 2020

Library of Congress Catalog Card Number pending
ISBN 978-1-5362-1674-5

21 22 23 24 25 26 APS 10 9 8 7 6 5 4 3 2 1

Printed in Humen, Dongguan, China

This book was typeset in Sabon.
The illustrations were done in watercolor and colored pencil.

Candlewick Press
99 Dover Street
Somerville, Massachusetts 02144

www.candlewick.com

ANNIE LUMSDEN,
the Girl from the Sea

DAVID ALMOND

illustrated by
Beatrice Alemagna

CANDLEWICK PRESS

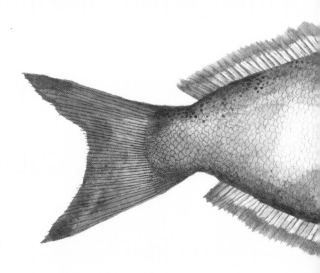

My mother says that all things can be turned to tales. When she said it first I thought she meant tales like fish tails, but I was wrong. She meant tales like this, tales that are stories. But this tale of mine is very like a fish tail too.

This is about me and my mum, and where we come from. And it's about the man who came one sunlit day and took the picture that hangs on the wall by my bed and shows the truth of me. His name was Benn. So this little tale of mine is some of his tale too.

I'm Annie Lumsden and I live with my mum in a house above the jetsam line on Stupor Beach. I'm thirteen years old and growing fast. I have hair that drifts like seaweed when I swim. I have eyes that shine like rock pools. My ears are like scallop shells. The ripples on my skin are like the ripples on the sand when the tide has turned back again. At night I gleam and glow like the sea beneath the stars and moon. Thoughts dart and dance inside like little minnows in the shallows. They race and flash like mackerel farther out. My wonderings roll in the deep like seals. Dreams dive each night into the dark like dolphins do, and break out happy and free into the morning light. These are the things I know about myself and that I see when I look in the rock pools at myself. They are the things that I see when I look at the picture the man from America gave to me before he went away.

Our house is a shack and is wooden, white, and salty.
We have a room each at the back with a bed each and a
cupboard each and a chair each. We have a kitchen just
like everybody has and a bathroom just like everybody
has. From the kitchen window we can see the village
past the dunes—the steeple of St. Mungo's Church,
the flag on top of Stupor Primary School, the
chimney pot on the Slippery Eel. At the front
of the shack is the room with the big wide
window that looks out across the rocks
and rock pools and the turning sea
toward the rocky islands. There
are many tales about the
islands. Saints lived on one
of them long ago. Another
of them has an ancient
castle on a rock. It's said
that mermaids used

to live out there, and sing sailors to their doom. We are in the north. It is very beautiful. They say it's cold here, especially the water, but I know nothing else, so it isn't cold to me. Nor to Mum, who loves this place too. She was brought up in the city, but ever since she was a girl she knew her happiness would be found by the sea.

We have a sandy garden with a rickety fence, and
in the garden are patterns of seashells and rocks that
mum has painted with lovely faces. Mum sells models
made from shells—sailing ships and mermaids'
thrones and fancy cottages—in The Lyttle Gyfte
Shoppe next to the Slippery Eel. She sells her painted
rocks there too. When I was little, I thought that
these rocks were the faces of sisters and brothers and
friends that had been washed up by the sea for me.
This made Mum laugh.

"No, my darling, they are simply rocks."

Then she lifted one of the rocks to her face and
showed how all things, even rocks that have lain
forever on an ordinary beach, can be made to turn
to tales.

"Hello," she whispered to this rock, which bore the
face of a sweet dark-haired little boy on it.

"Hello," it whispered back in such a soft, sweet voice.

"What is your name?" Mum said.

"My name is Septimus Samuel Swift," replied the
rock, and Mum held it close to her lips and let it look at
me as it told its tale of being the seventh son of a seventh
son and of traveling with pirates to Madagascar and
fighting with sea monsters in the Sea of Japan.

"Was that you that spoke the words?" I asked.

She winked and smiled.

"How could you think such a thing?" she said.

And she stroked my hair and set off singing a
sea shanty, the kind she sings on folk nights in the
Slippery Eel.

She finds tales everywhere—in grains of
sand she picks up from the garden, in puffs
of smoke that drift out from the chimneys of
the village, in fragments of smooth timber
or glass in the jetsam. She will ask them,
"Where did you come from? How did you
get here?" And they will answer her in
voices very like her own, but with new lilts
and squeaks and splashes in them that show
they are their own. Mum is good with tales.
Sometimes she visits Stupor Primary School
and tells them to the young ones. I used to
sit with the children and listen. The teachers
there, Mrs. Marr and Miss Malone, were
always so happy to see me again. "How
are you getting on?" they asked while the
children giggled and whispered, "She's
dafter than ever."

Long ago, they tried me at Stupor Primary School. It didn't work. I couldn't learn. Words in books stayed stuck to the page like barnacles. They wouldn't turn themselves to sound and sense for me. Numbers clung to their books like limpets. They wouldn't add, subtract, or multiply for me.

The children mocked and laughed. The teachers were
gentle and kind but soon they started to shake their heads
and turn away from me. They asked Mum to come in
for a chat. I'd been assessed, they said. Stupor Church of
England Primary School couldn't give me what I needed.
There was another school in another place where there
were other children like me. I stood at the window that
day while they talked at my back. I looked across the
fields behind the school toward the hidden city where that
other place would be. It broke my heart to think that I
must spend my days so distant from my mum and from
the sea. "It's for the best," said Mrs. Marr. That was a
momentous moment, the moment of my first fall.

My legs went weak beneath me and I tumbled to the floor and the whole world went watery and dark, and wild watery voices sang sweetly in my brain and called me to them. I came out of it to find Mum weeping over me and shaking me and screaming my name like I had drifted a million miles away, and the teacher yelling for help into the phone.

I reached up and caught Mum's falling tears.

"It's all right," I whispered sweetly to her. "It was lovely, Mum."

And it was. And I wanted it to happen again. And soon it did. And did again.

There followed months of trips to hospitals and visits to doctors and many, many tries to go past my strangeness and to find the secrets and the truth in me. There were lights shone deep into my eyes, blood sucked out of me, wires fixed to me, questions asked of me. There were stares and glares and pondering and wondering, and medicines and needles, and much talk coming out of many flapping mouths, and much black writing written on much white paper. I was wired wrong. The chemicals that flowed in me were wrong. My brain was an electric storm. There had been damage from disease, from a bang on the head, damage at my birth. It ended with a single doctor, Dr. John, in a single room with Mum and me.

"There is something wrong with Annie," said Dr. John.

"Something?" asked my mum.

"Yes," said Dr. John. He scratched his head. "Something. But we don't know what the something is so we haven't got a name for it."

And we were silent. And I was very pleased. And Mum hugged me.

And Dr. John said, "All of us are mysteries, even to us white-coated doctors. And some of us are a bit more of a puzzle than the rest of us."

He smiled into my eyes. He winked.

"You're a good girl, Annie Lumsden," he said.

"She is," said Mum.

"What's the thing," said Dr. John, "that you like best in the whole wide world?"

And I answered, "My mum is that thing. That, and splashing and swimming like the fishes in the sea."

"Then that's good," he said. "For unlike most of us, you have the things you love close by you. And you have them there on little Stupor Beach. Be happy. Go home."

So we went home.

A teacher, Miss McLintock, came each Tuesday. I stayed daft.

We went back to Dr. John each six weeks or so. I stayed a puzzle.

And we walked on the beach; we sat in the sandy garden. Mum painted her rocks and glued her shells, and told her tales and sang her shanties. I swam and swam, and we were happy.

"I sometimes think," I said one day, "I should have been a fish."

"A fish?"

"Aye. Sometimes I dream I've got fins and a tail."

"Goodness gracious!" said Mum.

She jumped up and lifted my T-shirt and looked at my spine.

"What's there?" I said.

She kissed me.

"Nowt, my little minnow," she said.

She looked again.

"Thank goodness for that," she said.

I fell many, many times. It happened in the salty shack,
in the sandy garden, on the sandy beach. My legs would
lose their strength and I would tumble, and the whole
of everything would turn watery, and it was like I really
turned from Annie Lumsden into something else—
to a fish or a seal or a dolphin. And when the world
turned back into sand and rocks and shacks
and gardens, I would find Mum sitting close
by, watching over me, waiting for
me to return, and she'd
smile and say,

"Where've you been, my little swimmer?" I'd tell her I'd been far away beneath the sea to places of coral and shells and beautifully colored fish, and she'd smile and smile to hear the words loosened from my tongue as I told my traveling tales. At first, Mum was scared that I would fall and lose myself when I was in the water, and that I would drown and be taken from her, but we came to know that it did not, and would never, happen, for in the water I am truly as I am—Annie Lumsden, seal girl, fish girl, dolphin girl, the girl who cannot drown.

Then there came the sunlit day, the day of Benn.
I lay on the warm sand at Mum's side. My body and
brain were reforming themselves after a fall. Every time
it happened, it was like being born again, like coming
out from dark and lovely water and crawling into the

world like a little new thing. She was gently stroking my
seaweed hair, and we were lost in wonder at the puzzle
of myself and the mystery of everything that is and ever
was and ever will be. I gazed at her and asked, "Mum,
tell me where I come from."

And she started to tell me a tale I knew so well, ever
since I was a little one.

"Once," she said, "when I was walking by the sea,
I saw a fisherman."

It was the old familiar tale. A man was fishing on
the beach, casting his line far out into the water. A
handsome man, in green waterproofs and green wellies.
A hardworking man from far down south, taking a
break at Stupor Beach. Mum passed by. They got to
talking. He said he loved the wildness of the north.
They got to drinking and dancing in the Slippery Eel.
He listened to Mum singing her shanties. He called her a
wild northern lass. He wasn't a bad man, not really, just
a bit careless and a bit feckless. He stayed a while then
quickly went away. He was searched for and never was
found. Charles, his name was, or he said it was. To tell
the truth, he wouldn't have made a decent daddy. It was
better like this, just Mum and me.

But that day I put my finger to her lips.

"No," I told her. "Not that old one. I know that one."

"But it's true."

"Tell me something with a better truth in it, something that works out the puzzle of me."

"Turn you into a tale?"

"Aye. Turn me to a tale."

She winked.

"I didn't want to tell you this," she said. "Will you keep it secret?"

"Aye," I said.

She leant over and looked at my back and stroked my spine.

"Nowt there," she said. "But maybe it's time to tell the truth at last."

And I lay there on the sand beneath the sun, and the
sea rolled and turned close by, and seagulls cried, and the
breeze lifted tiny grains of sand and scattered them on me.
And Mum's fingers moved on me and she breathed and
sighed and her voice started to flow over me and into me
as sweet as any song, and it found in me a different Annie
Lumsden; an Annie Lumsden that fitted with my fallings,
my dreams, my body, and the sea.

"I was swimming," she murmured. "It was summer, morning, very early—milky white sky, not a breath of wind, water like glass. Most of the world was deep asleep. Not a soul to be seen but a man in the dunes with a dog a quarter of a mile away. Nowt on the sea except a single dinghy slipping northward. Gannets high, high up and little terns darting back and forth into the water for fish, and nervy oystercatchers by the rock pools. The tide had turned, and it went back nearly soundless, just a gentle lovely hissing as it drained away; and all around, the secrets of the sea were given up—the rocks, the pools, the weeds, the darting creatures and the crawling and the scuttling creatures, the million grains of sand. And as I swam I was drawn backward and outward toward the islands, and farther from the line of jetsam and my things. Rocks began appearing all around. A great field of seaweed was exposed nearby, with stems as thick as children's arms and long brown rubbery leaves."

"Were you young?"

"Fourteen years younger than I am today. A young woman, and strong, with strong, smooth swimming muscles on my shoulders. My things were high up on the beach beyond the jetsam—a red plastic bag, a green towel laid out. I remember as I swam and dived and drifted that I felt stunned, almost hypnotized.

I kept trying to look back to the red and green, to remind myself that the solid world was the world I'd come from and that I must swim back again."

She smiled at me.

"You know that feeling?"

I smiled.

"You know I know that feeling."

"And as I drifted I felt the first touch on me."

"The touch?"

"A gentle tender touch. At first I told myself it was the shifting of the seaweed, or the flicker of a little fish fin. But then it came again, like something touching, deliberately touching. Something moved beneath. It moved right under me. A flickering swimming thing, slow and smooth. And it was gone. Then I was suddenly cold, and tiredness and hunger were in me. I stayed calm. I swam breaststroke slowly for the shore. I knelt in the wet sand there and told myself that I'd been wrong, I'd been deceived. I looked back. The sea was empty. I started to walk up the slope of wet sand toward my things. A bird screamed. I looked back again. A little tern hung dancing in the air close behind me, beak pointing down toward the water. It screamed again, then wheeled away as the man appeared from the brown-leaved weed."

"The man?" I whispered.

"He was slender, but with great shoulders on him. Hair slick like weed. Skin smooth and bright like sealskin. He crouched at the water's edge, poised between the land and sea. He cupped his hands and drank the sea. He raised his eyes toward the low milky sun and lowered them again. I could not, dared not, move. I saw the fin folded along his back."

"The fin?"

"I saw his webbed fingers, his webbed toes. His eyes were huge and dark and shining. He laughed, as if the moment brought him great joy. He cupped his hands again and poured water over himself. Then he raised his eyes and looked at me, and after a moment of great stillness in us both, he left the sea and came to me."

"You ran away?"

"There seemed no threat in him, no danger. I looked along the beach. The man with his dog in the dunes was a world away. The man with the fin came out. He knelt a yard away from me."

"Did he speak?"

"There was a sound from him, a splashing sound, like water rather than air was moving in his throat."

"What was he?"

"A mystery. A secret of the sea. He was very beautiful.
I saw in his eyes he thought I was beautiful too."

I looked into my mother's eyes. What did I see there?
The delight of memories or the delight of her imaginings?

"He was my father?" I whispered.

Her eyes were limpid pools.

"That was the first day," she said. "We moved no closer to each other. We did not touch. I saw the water drying on him, leaving salt on his beautiful skin. When he saw this, he lowered himself into the field of weed again and he was gone. But he came back again on other early milky mornings when the sea was calm. The last day he came, he stayed an hour with me. He came onto the land. We stayed in the shade beneath the rocks. I poured water from the rock pools over him. He was very beautiful, and his liquid voice was very beautiful."

"He was my father?"

"I touched his fin, his webs, his seaweed hair that day.
I remember them still against my fingers. That last day
we had to hurry back to the water. Despite the rock-pool
water, his skin was drying out, his voice was coarse, his
eyes were suddenly touched with dread. We ran back
to the water. He sighed as he lowered himself into the
water. We looked at each other, he from within the sea,
I from without. He reached out of the sea to me. His
hand was dripping wet, and in it was a shell—this shell."

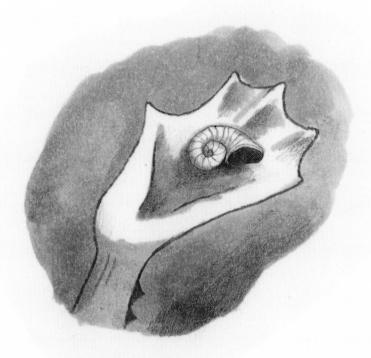

She opened her palm. In it was a seashell.

"Then he swam away."

I took the shell from her. It was as ordinary as any seashell, as beautiful as any seashell.

"I'll cut the story short," she said. "Nine months later you were born."

"And it's true?"

"And yes, it's—"

We heard a click. We turned. A man was standing
close by. He held a camera to his face. He lowered it.
"Forgive me," he said.

He moved toward us.
"But you were so lovely, the
two of you there. It was just
like the girl had been washed
up by the sea."
We said nothing, were still
lost in the tale that Mum
had told.

"Name's Benn," he said. "I'm passing through. Staying at your Slippery Eel. Came to take pictures of your islands."

He asked to be forgiven again. He took our silence for coldness, a desire to be left alone. He bowed, continued on his way.

"Please," said Mum.

He paused, looked back at us.

"We have few pictures of ourselves," she said. "Could we have the one you've taken today?"

He grinned, and we came back fully into the world, and Mum asked him into our sandy garden for tea.

He told us of his travels, of faraway cities and mountains and seas. He said he loved the feeling of moving through the world, light and free, moving through other people's stories. Sometimes, he said, when he got his photographs home, they were like images from dreams and legends. He laughed with delight at Stupor Bay. He swept his hands toward the sea and the islands.

"Who'd've guessed a place like this was waiting for me."

We said we'd hardly ever moved from this place, and for the first time, as I looked at Benn, I found myself thinking that one day we might move away.

He told us about America, and the kids called Maggie and Jason.

"You have the perfect gifts for them," he said.

He bought a rock painted with the face of a grinning angel and the seashell model of a mermaid.

He sipped his tea and ate his scone. He took more
photographs of us and of the shack and the islands.

"I always take home tales as well," he said.

He winked at Mum.

"You look like you might know a tale or two."

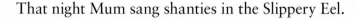

That night Mum sang shanties in the Slippery Eel.
I sat with Benn and drank lemonade
and nibbled crisps. Between the
songs he told me of all the seas
he'd seen around the world.
He dipped the tip of his
finger into his beer.

"An atom of the water in
this," he said, "was one
day in the Sea of Japan."
He dipped his finger
again. "And an atom of
this was in the Bay of
Bengal. All seas flow
into each other."
He licked his finger,
laughed. "And
into us."

I swigged my lemonade. I felt the Baltic Sea and the Yellow Sea and the Persian Gulf pour through me. Rain pattered on the window at our backs. Mum's voice danced around the music of a flute. We joined in with the choruses. We tapped the rhythms on the table. Benn drank and told me of his home and his family so many miles away.

"I'm happy when I'm there," he said. "But then I travel, and I find so many places to be happy in."

Mam's singing ended and she sat between me and Benn, and her voice was edged with laughter. At closing time we stood outside. The rain had stopped, the clouds had dispersed, the moon was out. The sea thundered on the shore.

"I'll do those pics tonight," he said. "Use night time as a dark room."

He touched Mum's face. He told her she was beautiful. I turned away. They whispered. I think they kissed.

The man with the fin
surfaced in my dreams. I spoke
the watery words for "dad." He
spoke the airy words for "daughter." We
swam together to southern seas of colored
fish and coral, to northern seas of icebergs and
whales. We swam all night from sea to sea to sea
to sea, and when I woke, the sun was up and there
were already voices in the garden.

"Come and see," said Mum when I appeared at the door.

Her eyes were wide and shining.

"Come and see," said Benn.

I walked barefoot through the sand. There were photographs scattered on the garden table. Mum held another photograph against her breast.

"You ever see one of these things develop?" said Benn.

I shook my head.

"At first the things in them are seen like secret things, through liquid—like secret creatures glimpsed beneath the sea. They're seen by a strange pale light that shines just like a moon." He narrowed his eyes, gazed at me, smiled. "These are the secrets I glimpsed last night, Annie Lumsden."

Then he stepped away from us, faced the islands, left us alone.

I sifted through the photos on the table: Mum and me, the garden, the shack, the islands. Mum still held the other to her breast.

"Look, Annie," she said.

She bit her lip as she tilted the photograph over at last and let me see.

There we were, Mum and me at the water's edge. Like Benn said, it was like I was something washed up by the sea, like Mum was reaching out to help me up, to help me to be born. I saw how seaweedy my hair truly was, how sealy my skin was. Then I looked away, looked back again, but it was true. A fin was growing at my back. Narrow, pale, half formed, like it was just half grown, but it was a fin.

Mum touched me there now, below my neck, between my shoulders. She traced the line of my spine. I touched where she touched, but we touched only me.

"Nothing there?" I whispered.

"Nothing there."

I traced the same line on the photograph. I looked at Benn, straight and tall, facing the islands and the sea.

"Could Benn . . . ?" I started.

"How could you think such a thing?" said Mum.

I looked at her.

"So the tale was true?" I said.

She smiled into my eyes.

"Aye. The tale was true."

And I pushed the photograph into her hand, and ran away from her and ran past Benn, and ran into the waves and didn't stop until I'd plunged down deep and burst back up again and swum and felt the joy of the fin quivering at my back, supporting me, helping me forward.

I looked back, saw Mum and Benn at the water's edge, hand in hand.

"You saw the truth!" I yelled.

"And the truth can set you free!" Benn answered back.

He went away soon afterward. He said he had a boxer to see in London and maybe an actress in Milan, and there was a war he needed to attend to in the Far East, and . . . He shrugged. Must seem a shapeless, aimless life to folk like us, he said.

"You get yourself to the States one day," he said to me. "You go and see my Maggie."

I gulped.

"I will," I said, and as I said it I believed it.

"Good. And you can be sure she'll know your tale by then."

We waited with him for a taxi outside the Slippery Eel. He had his painted rock and his shell mermaid. He held Mum tight and kissed her.

I held the shell that Mum had given me.

"Can I . . . ?" I said to her.

She smiled and nodded.

"It's for you," I said to Benn. "And then for Maggie."

He held it to his ear.

"I hear the roaring of the sea. I hear the whisper of its secrets. I hear the silence of its depths." He winked. "I know it's very precious, Annie. I'll keep it safe."

And he kissed me on the brow. Then the taxi came, and the man from America left Stupor Bay.

Afterward things were never quite the same. Things that'd seemed fixed and hard and hopeless started to shift. Words stopped being barnacles. Numbers were no longer limpets. I started to feel as free on land as I did in the sea. I fell less and less. Miss McLintock started talking about trying me in a school again. Was it to do with Mum's tales and Benn's photograph? One day I dared to tell Dr. John about the man with the fin. He laughed and laughed. I dared to show him Benn's picture and he laughed again. Then he went quiet.

"Sometimes," he said, "the best way to understand how to be human is to understand our strangeness."

He asked to look at my back. He peeped down beneath the back of my collar.

"Nothing there?" I said.

"Yes. There is an astonishing thing there. A mystery. And sometimes the biggest mystery of all is how a mystery might help to solve another mystery." Then he laughed again. "Pick the sense out of that!" he said.

He smiled.
"Come back
in a year's time,
Annie Lumsden,"
he said.

And, of course, it was all to do with simple growing up, with being thirteen, heading for fourteen and beyond. And it was to do with having a mum who thought there was nothing strange in loving a daughter who might be half a creature from the sea.